LEGACY TAKEDOWN

BY

Eidahs

COVER BY

BINKY INK

BINKY INK

THE LITERARY ARM OF BINKY PRODUCTIONS

WWW.BINKYPRODUCTIONS.COM/SHORT STORIES

Published in 2024 by Binky Ink

ISBN: 978-1-7382829-2-0

Table of Contents

Danno entered the casino where his father had instructed him to go. *Finally.* He was being trusted with something big, he knew, though his father had not told him the details. He had merely told Danno to go retrieve the package and then bring it to him at the business hotel.

Since his father, brother and he had moved to North America, Danno had been left in the dark regarding much of his father's affairs, being the youngest son. Now he was in his early thirties, wondering what he was going to do with his life if his brother were to inherit the business.

Danno had always wanted to be part of his father's hotel chain, had wanted to learn how his father managed to negotiate so many deals that had made him the billionaire he was today. And yet Danno felt something was missing.

He had turned to security and had trained to bodyguard his father as any loyal son would. He had worked hard to show his father that, just like his brother, he was ready to take on more responsibilities with the business.

'Good evening, Mr. Igoshima,' a tall burly fellow said. 'Right this way.'

The American led Danno to a door at the back and into an elevator that took them down a few levels. He then led Danno into a backroom where stood two men, armed with repeaters, hovering around a computer.

Danno noted the lack of security cameras down on this floor, and an uneasy feeling crept up his spine.

Danno's escort bowed politely and left the three men alone to confer.

'Mr. Igoshima,' one who had a southern accent said, 'your father told us to expect you.'

'Yes. I'm here to pick up the package,' asserted Danno. Though he still had no clue what the package was.

'Your father will find that she matches all the specifications indicated by him, except for a few details,' said the other man. He winced. 'But I assure you, your father will be more than pleased with her.'

Her? Danno wondered. 'May I see her?'

'Certainly, Mr. Igoshima.'

The Americans led Danno through another door to a small room where sat a woman, wrists bound behind her, ankles bound, and mouth gagged.

Danno froze, his heart rising to his throat. He balled his hands into fists.

'What is this?' he hissed. 'This is the package?'

The American men winced further. 'We apologise that she is not as young as the others we provided,' one of them began. Danno clenched his jaw, feeling disgusted at the realisation before him. 'But I promise she will not disappoint.'

Danno slowly walked to the woman. She looked no more than a few years older than him, perhaps mid-thirties, with dark wavy hair falling below her shoulders; her face was stricken with sweat.

Danno gently removed the gag from her mouth. 'What is your name?'

'Aliana,' she replied.

Danno swallowed, knowing instinctively what he had to do. After years of trying to prove to his father that he was just as worthy as his brother, he now understood what this life meant if he walked down that same path.

'Aliana,' breathed Danno, 'close your eyes for me. Can you do that?'

She nodded and closed her eyes.

Danno whirled on the two men, whipping his gun up, and shot them in quick succession in the chest. They fell dead before they knew what was happening.

Danno spun around to face Aliana. 'I'm going to get you out of here.' He quickly unbound her hands and legs. 'Are you hurt?'

'No,' Aliana replied, looking alarmed.

'Good.' Danno took her by the hand.

'Are you not going to bring me to your father?' asked Aliana. She had a slight accent, Danno reckoned from Mexico. It was lovely.

Danno motioned the two dead men with his gun. 'I can't.' Confusion reflected in Aliana's eyes. 'I had no idea what my father was up to. I can't bring you to him knowing what he does.'

'There are other girls – I heard them talking about them – all sorts of nationalities, all immigrants.'

Danno felt sick to his stomach. He brought his gun hand up to his mouth, cursing in Japanese. That's when he realised this was a test, and his father would come after him if he set Aliana free. What would Mr. Igoshima Senior do with his son who had so readily betrayed him after vying for his approval all his life?

Danno's hand tightened around Aliana's as he led her out of the room and through the other chamber. He shot the security guard by the elevator.

Once inside, he turned to Aliana. 'I'm bringing you to a safehouse.'

'Won't your father know about it?' objected Aliana.

'No, not that one. That one's mine.' His eyes drifted from Aliana's face to her body and back, meeting her gaze. 'A beautiful woman like you doesn't deserve to be taken captive and treated like property.'

A small smile curled on the side of Aliana's mouth and Danno's heart skipped a beat. 'Didn't peg the son of a human trafficker for a hero.'

'Well, I don't think of myself as a criminal and . . .' Danno paused. 'I'm sorry this has happened to you. I promise I'll keep you safe. You'll need to stay at the safehouse until I figure out what to do, what I *can* do.' He cursed again. 'My father is going to be furious. He's going to kill me . . . literally.'

'You really had no idea?'

Danno shook his head.

He led Aliana through the casino, making it look like she was his property, acting as his brother had with every date he'd sauntered around with.

Now Danno knew how both his father and brother always found such young women to prance around with. Danno also suspected many of the staff workers, who coincidentally were all female, also of various nationalities, had also been captured and trafficked.

Danno hurried to his car and drove as quickly as he could to the safehouse. Once inside, he finally let out a shaking breath and put his gun down on the bed, hands trembling.

'You are in shock,' Aliana remarked.

'And you're not?' demanded Danno, anger and concern swirling inside of him.

'I'm made of tough stuff.'

Danno walked to her, his hands instinctively going to her arms. 'Did they hurt you? Touch you? Make you do anything you didn't want?

'They knocked me out good but it's nothing I can't handle,' replied Aliana.

'You say that as though you weren't just taken and sold to a billionaire to serve him as his slave!'

Aliana downcast her eyes. 'You are not at all what I was expecting.'

'What were you expecting?' asked Danno, curious.

'I was expecting to be taken to your father and commanded to do what he wanted of me. Maybe be roughed about a bit by the one taking me to him.'

She said it like it was fact and Danno's kindness was a novelty, which only made his heart go out to her even more. He didn't know what it was about this woman, or perhaps it was the adrenaline of discovering a shockingly disgusting truth that had always been hidden from him, but Danno could not quell the feeling that this woman was special.

Danno walked over to the computer at the desk and began to frantically type away, standing at the keyboard and peering down at the screen. Aliana joined him, cocking her brow.

'They mentioned other girls, younger ones, you say?' began Danno. 'I need to know how many? For how long? Why I never knew before now?'

Aliana let out a small laugh. Danno paused, lifting his head to her quickly. She smiled. 'Is it not obvious why they never told you before?' She motioned to him with her hand, then herself, and then the computer. 'You don't have the stomach for it.'

'Nor do I have the heart to see innocent women being taken advantage of and treated so cruelly,' admitted Danno.

'They must have known that.'

'Perhaps.' Danno returned his attention to the computer. 'There.' He pointed at what he'd found.

'Records of other women, young girls, some of them barely adults.' His stomach rose and he had to clamp down the nauseating feeling again. He swallowed hard. 'This has been going on for years, decades. Since I was a boy.' He closed his eyes. 'And my brother is part of it.'

'At least you're not,' Aliana said gently.

'I don't know what I'm supposed to do now that I know.' Danno felt overwhelmed with emotion. 'I want to help them all. I just don't know how.' He stared at the screen where it indicated that so many of the girls had been escorted to his father by one of the Igoshima heirs.

Aliana pointed at the screen. 'Is that you or your brother?' she demanded. 'Because from where I'm standing, it could be you.' She took a step back. Danno's heart sank at the realisation that he had not earned her trust and of what he must look like to her. 'You pretending with me, or something?'

'No, I swear.' Danno walked over to her, pleading. 'I promise, I had no idea about any of this. Please believe me, Aliana.' He couldn't explain why it was important to him for her to believe him, but he just needed her to know he was not that kind of man. 'I am not that kind of man.'

Aliana glanced at the gun on the bed. 'Trusting of you to leave that lying around. Bring me here, tell me I can't leave because it's too dangerous. Perhaps you want me to yourself.'

'Not like that,' Danno blurted. He closed his eyes, turning his head and cursing himself for his candour. 'That's not . . . I realise how that sounds.'

'So you wouldn't want to take advantage of me?' Aliana crossed her arms.

'I promise,' Danno asserted, meeting her gaze. 'I just want to understand . . . I don't want to be like him anymore. All my life I thought I did. With what I just found out, I feel disgusted, sickened,' he disdained. 'I want to save all of them. I just don't know how.'

'Take me to your father, then.'

'What?'

'Take me to your father,' Aliana repeated. 'I can help you help them. I'm older than the rest of them, more resourceful.'

'But my father will force you to—' Just the thought threatened to make Danno spill the contents of his stomach.

'I can take care of myself,' Aliana assured him. 'But you want to find the other girls, yes? Free them? There are some half my age on there.' She pointed at the screen. 'Take me to your father. I can be . . . your woman on the inside.'

Danno took a step closer to her, suddenly feeling protective. 'If either of them lay one hand on you,' he breathed gruffly. He stopped. 'I'm sorry. I don't know where this is coming from.'

Aliana suppressed a laugh. 'You're sweet, you know that? Too sweet for your own good.' Her eyes met his. 'I think if we help each other, we can save the other girls.' She paused. 'Do you want to stop your father's criminal activities?'

'Yes!' Danno asserted without needing to think about it. 'I thought I wanted his business but . . .'

'Perhaps you can have it and change it. But first let's find those girls and save them.'

Danno took a moment to think.

'Are you certain?' he asked. 'There's no going back once I bring you to my father.' Realisation came to Danno and his heart dropped. 'I killed those men. What am I supposed to tell him?'

'Tell him they were roughing me up, they were going to spoil me for him. That as his loyal son, you couldn't let them do that.'

Danno had to admit, it was a viable plan. The fact that there had been no security cameras played in his favour. 'You're definitely something, you know that?' he said, admiring her determination.

Aliana smiled, looking like there was a confident woman hiding beneath the torn blouse and tousled hair.

'All right.' Danno didn't like the plan – he hated it – but it was the best they had, and it was what would keep him alive for now, though it probably wasn't the safest for Aliana. Even so, the resolve on her face and in her voice gave Danno the courage to face whatever came next.

Aliana nodded and they headed out of the safe-house. Danno drove to the hotel and when they reached the penthouse, he told his father the fabricated story as Aliana had suggested he do. He had bound her wrists again, loosely, and now unbound them in front of his father.

'She's too old,' his father complained. 'I can't believe they thought this would please me.'

'Can the young ones cook?' asked Aliana. 'Clean?'

'You will speak only when spoken to,' Danno's father threatened.

'Mr. Igoshima,' Aliana purred, taking a step towards him and playing with her hair. Something about it made Danno tense up. 'I'm certain that my skills and experience could serve you where one so young could not.' She trailed a finger along Mr. Igoshima Senior's arm, her eyes never leaving his.

Danno's father's lips pursed thoughtfully before curling into a predatory smile that tightened the grip Danno felt in his stomach.

'Perhaps I can test this one and see if she proves herself useful,' he conceded. He turned to Danno. 'Well done, my son. You may leave us.'

Danno's heart palpitated for a moment. He slowly backed away and gave his father a bow. 'Yes, father.'

Danno stole one last glance at Aliana, his heart quickly sinking, and left them.

<u>Part 2</u>

Aliana's eyes never left Mr. Igoshima Senior's, and she made sure to keep her smile in place, no matter how dirty she felt just looking at the man. His sleazy smile came with a bit of drool. He took her by the hand and bid her to follow him to where she would be staying and taking care of his needs when he slept in that room.

This told her that other girls probably were kept in other such rooms. Mr. Igoshima led Aliana to a penthouse suite with a beautiful view. It was near morning now, so Mr. Igoshima excused himself and instructed Aliana to be ready for him tonight.

Aliana took to cleaning the suite, dusting off the furniture, cleaning the couch and rugs, moving everything to clean under it and get at all the dust in every room of the suite.

When Mr. Igoshima arrived that evening, he was impressed. Aliana curtsied politely, then made point to catch herself and bowed before she bid Mr. Igohimi sit on the freshly vacuumed couch.

'Bring me a tall bourbon.'

'Right away, Mr. Igoshima.' Aliana poured him his drink and sat next to him as she placed it on the small table in front of the couch. She kept her knees together but angled them towards M. Igoshima to give the semblance of interest. 'Long stressful day?'

'That would be one way of putting it,' Mr. Igoshima replied.

Without invitation, she stood and began to massage his shoulders, carefully kneading his neck. He relaxed in her touch, groaning like a cat and melting like putty in her hands.

'When we . . .' she began, after he'd finished his second drink, while massaging his back, 'do you always like to film it?'

Mr. Igoshima chuckled. 'Found them, did you?'

'Difficult not to, when cleaning.' She pressed on a tender part and massaged gently. Mr. Igoshima moaned pleasurably. 'You like to record audio too?'

'No audio,' replied Mr. Igoshima. 'But if you're up for it, we can angle the cameras so that when I rewatch later I can have an even better view of you.'

'That sounds like an excellent idea,' Aliana cooed.

Aliana moved back to his neck, massaging in circular motions that elicited a yawn from Mr. Igoshima. She found the pressure point she was looking for, carefully ensuring that to him it would only seem as though he dozed off to sleep. She pressed and he was out cold.

Aliana took a step back. She moved Mr. Igoshima to a lying position on the couch and began to clean in a safe corner of the suite.

'I count five security cameras,' Aliana muttered. 'No audio, as you heard. No sign of any of the other girls yet. I suspect they're being kept in individual suites like this one but I can't say if all of them are as lucky as me. Suite is . . . luxurious enough. I get my own bed too.'

'Well done, Sanchez,' came the voice on the other end of the earpiece – her boss, Anderson. 'Feeling safe? Nothing untoward occurred?'

'I'm all good, thanks,' replied Aliana. 'You would have heard anyway.'

'We've done more research and digging,' Anderson went on. 'Turns out your boy, Danno, was never part of the past schemes. He's clean. See what you can find out from him the next time you speak with him.'

'*If* I get to speak to him again,' corrected Aliana.

'We've got agents shadowing the three Igoshimas, but so far only Igoshima Senior and his eldest son frequent that casino from where they get their girls. Digging into their pasts revealed the same. We've got a point of entry. We'll soon find who brings them the girls and where they take them from.'

'Good.' Aliana moved a mantel and dusted it off with the duster brush.

'Agent Sanchez, don't hesitate to do what you have to if any of them cross any lines.'

'I won't. Don't worry about me. I'll be fine.' She turned to make sure Mr. Igoshima was still snoring.

Then she lowered her voice and gave the coordinates she remembered of the safehouse. 'Gain access to that computer. You'll find records of the trafficking there with dates and names.'

* * *

The next morning, Aliana was up early with breakfast laid out for Mr. Igoshima. She had a new suit ironed out for him and set everything for him with a smile that told him she was happy to serve him. He seemed satisfied enough, despite his early night in.

'The others don't have this kind of initiative,' Mr. Igoshima complained. Or was it praise towards her? 'They always have to be told what to do. And then they don't smile their beautiful smiles as you do.'

'That's why you need a *woman*, Mr. Igoshima. Now,' she fixed up his collar, 'should I be expecting you tonight, or will you be visiting one of the others?'

'Don't expect me for a few nights, at least,' said Mr. Igoshima. 'Just keep the place tidy, and if you have visitors, treat them the same way you would me.'

Aliana put on her best smile, biting her lower lip, and purred. 'It will be my utmost pleasure.'

Mr. Igoshima chuckled. 'You know, I'm glad they found you. You've been well trained.'

Aliana kept her smile on, easily done from years of practice dealing with all sorts of people throughout her career. Mr. Igoshima left the suite.

'Ugh.' Eli, who was on the other end of the earpiece today, made a gagging sound. 'I think I just puked in my mouth.'

Aliana quickly turned away from the cameras. 'Don't make me laugh, Eli. I'm on a job.'

'Apologies. But today, you don't get the boss's serious remarks to keep you company but my quips.'

Over the course of several days, Aliana was able to report what she overheard or gathered from security guards passing outside the suite as she worked, humming from time to time when they visited her to inspect if she was doing her duty. She ensured to look like she was minding her own business, preparing meals and eating by herself most days and nights.

When Mr. Igoshima visited, she always ensured he was relaxed, too relaxed to take advantage of her. Aliana spoke to him in purrs and soothing tones, stroking his ego enough to make him complain about others when drunk enough. It all went back to the boss, and her fellow agents could do their work as she did hers.

Finally, one evening a soft knock came at the door before Danno entered the suite.

'Danno!' Aliana beamed at him. He was such a sweet man and she was happy to see him. 'I missed that handsome face of yours.'

Danno blushed significantly before he let out a self-conscious chuckle. 'I've been instructed to . . .' He hesitated. 'My father told me to choose any girl I wanted and enjoy her.'

Aliana cocked her brow, folding her arms. 'Is that so?'

'I mean, of course, I won't!' Danno quickly added. 'I won't sleep with you. I mean, not that I don't— You're a beautiful woman, Aliana, I . . .' He paused and sighed. 'I would not force you to do anything you would not want. I would never sleep with a woman without first taking her out on a date and showing my affection for her.'

'A perfect gentleman,' smiled Aliana. She sobered as Danno stepped further into the suite. 'Has it occurred to you that this might be another test? He might be expecting you to do as he would.'

'In that case, I will fail, and gladly.' Danno's eyes stayed on Aliana's and she felt a sudden flutter at the look in his eyes. 'I won't do it, not under these circumstances. Only under the right ones.'

Aliana couldn't help but smile mildly. 'And what would the right ones be?'

'Well first, I would take a woman to dinner,' began Danno, walking to the mantel and taking a bottle of bourbon whiskey. 'And I would greet her with flowers.' He poured himself a glass. 'Then I would take her for a romantic walk – women like those.' He turned to face Aliana. 'Then I would kiss you under the stars.'

'So your hypothetical woman is me?' inquired Aliana.

Danno blushed – he was cute when he blushed. He opened his mouth to speak but seemed at a loss. Aliana put him out of his misery.

'Then what would you wish to do with me tonight?'

He lifted the glass and offered it to Aliana. 'Have a drink with me?'

Aliana smiled. 'Gladly.'

* * *

After sharing that drink, Danno and Aliana chatted and carefully exchanged a few words regarding other girls before he left for the night.

Danno told Aliana there was a second basement where Danno had not been allowed to go, where he suspected the other girls were being kept, though he did confirm many had their own suites.

It was afternoon when the door burst open and in walked a man Aliana did not recognise. He slowly sauntered over to her, a hungry expression on his face. Aliana had the uncomfortable feeling that this was the more dangerous brother.

He smiled sinisterly. 'My father did say you were unique.'

'Mr. Igoshima.' Aliana bowed.

'Please. Hibiki.' He looked around. 'You are meticulous; you do your job well. But my father has not been able to care for you in the manner he promised you.'

'Really, it's no trouble at all,' Aliana insisted.

'And my brother obviously does not know how to woo.'

Aliana took a step back as Hibiki stepped closer, her heart racing. She swallowed, wanting to retort how Danno was much better at wooing because he was a genuinely good person.

Hibiki kept deliberately walking towards Aliana. 'I'm here to show you why we took you in.'

Aliana realised she had her back against the tall glass window. Hibiki was on her, grabbing her low-held wrists and pinning her against the window, pressing himself against her. She turned her head to the side.

'Please, Hibiki, I still have work to do before your father returns.'

'My father told me your work was to satisfy my needs.' His voice was a growl that sent an uncomfortable shiver down Aliana's spine.

He took her face in his fingers, squeezing her cheeks, and turned her head so she looked at him. 'And you will obey my commands, you old bitch.'

Aliana thrust her arms up and sent her knee into Hibiki's stomach. She slammed her elbow onto his shoulder, kicking his crotch. He groaned, bending over. She reached for his gun at his waist and slammed the butt of the gun onto his head hard. Hibiki fell to the ground, unconscious.

The door to the suite flung open and Danno ran in, panting and looking like he was ready to murder someone. He looked down at his brother, then back up at Aliana.

'What did he do to you?' he demanded, dashing to her side.

'Nothing. I didn't give him the chance.'

Danno let out a shaking breath.

'How did you know?' asked Aliana.

'I found the security footage,' replied Danno. He looked up at one of the cameras. 'They'll know what happened soon enough.'

Danno looked down at the gun in Aliana's hand and that's when she realised that he held her other hand, his thumb rubbing circles on her knuckles, and she welcomed the tingle it elicited.

'I'm sorry.' He let go.

'We better hurry, then.' Aliana bent and took a security badge from Hibiki's belt. 'I think I know how to gain access to the basement where the girls are being held.' She waved the key card at Danno.

He nodded, a determined look on his face. Together they ran out of the room, but before they could reach the elevator, a security detail intercepted them.

Danno skidded to a halt, stepping protectively in front of Aliana.

'Guns down, now!' he demanded.

'Sorry, Danno, but you failed your father's tests. You should have punished the hag when you found out what she'd done to your brother. Let this be a lesson to you to never interfere with the legacy of Mr. Igoshima.'

'She's not a hag,' Danno growled through his teeth.

Aliana grabbed Danno's hand and pulled him behind a corner as the two of them dodged a bullet. She shot at the security guard, then at another.

Danno shot at the third and fourth. A fifth came barreling towards them and Aliana thrust her elbow backwards into his ribs, spinning, and brought the butt of her gun to his head as Danno shot him in the stomach.

Panting, Danno looked up at Aliana, bewildered and awed. 'Where'd you learn to do that?'

'No time to explain. Elevator, now!'

Aliana took hold of Danno's hand and pulled him with her into the elevator. She pressed the button for the second basement level.

'Let's hope they don't cut power to this thing, it's a long way down,' breathed Aliana.

'We don't have much time before they catch on to what we're doing,' said Danno.

'They might move the girls – you need to get them out as quickly as possible before you get yourselves killed!' Anderson bellowed into Aliana's earpiece.

'Then get your asses here ASAP and we won't have that problem!' Aliana ordered. 'Sorry,' she added softly, looking at Danno. 'Let's start over.' She held out her hand. 'Aliana Sanchez, undercover agent.'

Danno chuckled, nodding. 'That's why you insisted I take you to my father.'

'Yes. Typically I go in with a whole new identity, but for this . . . Well, let's just say minimal cover worked to my advantage.'

'I consider myself lucky to have met the real you, then, despite everything.'

'And Sanchez, try to take Igoshima alive!'

'Alive might not be possible, the way things are going.' She paused. 'Sorry, them.' Danno merely chuckled. 'I'm sorry I had to lie.'

'No, don't be.' Danno smiled warmly. 'I see it, capable woman like you, wanting to help me save the other girls.'

His hand was back on hers, his thumb rubbing circles on her knuckles. Aliana wasn't even sure he knew he was doing it. She leaned and gave him a small peck on the cheek.

Danno blushed. 'What's that for?'

'For being a perfect gentleman with me.'

Danno's eyes darkened and his voice came out husky. 'If I'm being perfectly honest, it's hard to resist you.'

Danno leaned forward, pausing briefly, his lips grazed Aliana's and her breath hitched.

The elevator dinged and they reluctantly pulled apart, Danno's eyes indicating how unsatiated he felt.

They pressed their backs against the elevator wall, each of them on either side of the doors.

Aliana glanced at Danno. 'It's showdown time.'

The elevator doors parted and an onslaught of gunfire erupted, hitting the back of the elevator before it stopped.

Aliana and Danno looked one more time at each other and nodded before emerging and jumping into the fray.

<u>PART 3</u>

Danno rolled forward, refocusing his mind. He set aside the flutter from the near kiss and the excitement from Aliana's revelation that she was an undercover agent, and instead brought to the forefront his anger towards his father for his despicable schemes.

Coming to a crouch, he shot at one of his father's goons, then at the other. In his peripheral vision, he saw Aliana move along the wall and lunge at one of their attackers.

Danno grabbed the legs of another, tripping him, and shot him in the head. Danno leapt up to his feet, putting his bodyguard training to good use, and pulled the arm of another gunman, shoving him into his comrade. The two careened to the ground and Aliana and Danno each shot one of them simultaneously.

With the contingent of guards down, Danno instinctively took Aliana's hand and ran across the corridor. They found rooms, securely locked, with nothing but a small window in each door to peer inside from. Using Hibiki's keycard, Aliana unlocked the doors.

There were dozens of young women inside the scantily furnished rooms. These women were of all nationalities, talking in various languages trying to understand one another. Most of them were in their early twenties, some of them looked no older than sixteen, and all of them looked battered and bruised.

Danno clamped down the sudden urge to vomit.

Aliana was able to communicate with some of the girls in Spanish; others who understood her in English, translated into their language to their fellow captives.

'There's another elevator at the other end of the corridor. I believe it goes up to the ground floor,' expressed Danno.

'Danno!' bellowed Mr. Igoshima Senior, rage in his gritty voice.

Danno froze. His father's footsteps were hurried and heavy, coming from across the long hall.

Danno turned to Aliana. 'Get the girls to safety.'

'I'm not letting you face your father alone,' insisted Aliana.

'Someone has to get these girls out,' growled Danno. 'My father is mine to deal with.' He checked his gun clip and readied himself for the inevitable. He glanced down the hall. 'Father and brother,' he corrected himself.

'I'm coming back,' Aliana promised.

She hurriedly ushered the girls towards the other elevator, shooting any guards who came running towards them.

Danno turned towards his approaching father and brother and stalked towards them, gun held up at eye level, arm out in front of him, ready to pull the trigger on them.

Danno came face to face with them, several metres away, keeping his gun aimed at their heads. Mr. Igoshima Senior held his gun at his side. Hibiki held his by his face, resting his jaw and cheek on it, looking smug.

'I knew you were soft, Danno,' his brother chided, 'but I didn't think you'd be stupid enough to betray our father's legacy.'

'A legacy? Is that what you call it? Capturing innocent immigrants and using them as slaves? Abusing them, coercing them, so they will obey out of fear!? You're both disgusting. All my life, all I wanted was your approval, to be worthy of your praise. I was wrong to want it. Now I know what you truly are, father.'

'And what is that, son?' his father condescended.

'A monster!' seethed Danno. 'A disgusting monster.'

Mr. Igoshima chuckled. 'You should see your face, it's priceless. Contort it more and you'll get stuck in that position.'

'I'd rather that than be like you. How could you do such a thing?'

'I told you we should have kept him in the dark,' chided Hibiki.

'He would have found out eventually,' replied Mr. Igoshima.

Danno felt himself shaking with rage. He spat on the ground. 'I no longer want your legacy *or* your praise.'

'Are you disowning me, Danno? Careful what that might do to you.'

'I no longer want to be your son!' seethed Danno.

'This puts us at odds,' said Mr. Igoshima. 'We could have . . . worked something out. But now you give me no choice. This has to end with your death or mine. Except I know you, Danno. You're my son, I raised you. While you were good at defending and protecting, killing never came easily to you.'

Mr. Igoshima looked around at the bodies in the hallway. 'Heh, this is the most you've killed in your entire life.'

'You say that as though I should be ashamed of myself for it,' Danno spat back. 'I'm proud I never killed many people.'

'Are you truly going to kill me? Your own father?' asked Mr. Igoshima. 'Look at you, you're shaking. You can't even keep your arm still. You don't have the heart to pull the trigger on m—'

Danno shot his brother; the sound of the gunshot thundered through the hallway. Then, for a moment, there was silence, and Hibiki stared at Danno in shock before collapsing to the ground.

Danno aimed his gun at his father. 'Do you still think I can't do it?'

'Now you've gone and done it, Danno,' Mr. Igoshima hissed. He let out a series of expletives in Japanese, training his gun on Danno.

Danno lunged to the floor as his father shot at him repeatedly, and the bullets harmlessly whizzed above him.

Danno grabbed his father's legs, sending him to the ground with a loud thud. His father kicked Danno's hand and Danno's gun skittered across the floor. Mr. Igoshima punched Danno in the ribs – Danno returned a punch to his father's jaw.

Mr. Igoshima pressed his gun to Danno's throat, just under his chin. 'The price for betrayal is death, my son.'

Danno swiped his arm at his father's wrist with force and the shot ricocheted just beside Danno's head instead. Danno grabbed his father's wrist, wrestling with him to gain control of the gun.

Mr. Igoshima thrust the gun in Danno's face, hitting him hard in the nose but not enough to fracture it. Danno chopped his hand down on his father's wrist and the gun fell to the floor. He reached for it but his father punched down on his arm, hard. Danno yelled, pained, and the gun, in their scuffle, skittered out of reach.

Danno was pinned down beneath his father, unable to reach for the gun and unable to break free.

Mr. Igoshima's hands found Danno's throat and he began to squeeze. Danno groaned in pain, struggling to maintain airflow. His vision blurred as black dots sparkled before his eyes. He desperately tried to pry his father's hands from his throat to no avail.

With the last of his strength, Danno poked at Mr. Igoshima's eyes with his fingers.

'Argh!' Mr. Igoshima put a hand to his face, loosening his grip on Danno's throat.

Danno took advantage and shoved the man off him. Danno rolled onto his stomach. He grabbed the gun and shot once.

Blood began to drench his father's clothes at the stomach.

Danno shot again.

His father collapsed onto his back.

Danno rose to his feet, pointing the gun at Mr. Igoshima's head.

'Danno!' shouted Aliana, racing in, holding a gun levelled and pointed at Mr. Igoshima. 'Put the gun down – we need to take him in alive,' she ordered.

Danno clenched his teeth.

His father wheezed. 'Your mother, when she found out,' he managed through heavy breaths, 'met her fate.'

Danno felt his entire body vibrate with a deep and sudden rage at the admission from his father. He pulled back the gun's safety.

'Don't do it, Danno! You're not a killer. Let us deal with him, please.'

Danno snarled at his father. 'You're going to Hell!' He kicked him in the face, knocking him out.

Screaming his rage, Danno whipped the gun at the wall.

Many officers ran in and towards the two downed Igoshima men.

Danno placed his hands on the wall above his head, heaving, angry and yet relieved. He had not realised how frightened he'd been at the moment when he could have died. Now that it was over . . .

Danno felt a hand gently touch his arm. 'It's over,' Aliana said gently. Danno looked over his shoulder at her, feeling as though he was glaring at her, but on Aliana's face, Danno saw that she understood his anger was not towards her. 'They'll want to question you at the precinct.'

Danno nodded and pushed away from the wall. 'Then let's get that over with,' he said, his voice low.

* * *

By the time they were done questioning and processing him, night had passed and dawn had arrived. Danno was exhausted – he needed a good nap, and a good shower – but he was also relieved, calm even.

Danno stepped out of the office where he and the agents had sat discussing everything Danno knew and didn't know, and found Aliana speaking with another agent. The two were chuckling as the other one made some silly remark.

He clocked Danno and nudged Aliana who turned to Danno, smiling.

Danno walked over to Aliana. He hesitated but a moment before asking. 'Agent Sanchez, would you like to go to dinner with me?'

Aliana beamed at him. 'I'd love to.'

'Great. Uh, pick you up at six?' He paused. 'P.M.,' he added, realising it was barely 6:00 a.m.

'You don't know where to pick me up.'

'I'm sure you'll tell me?' Danno surmised, confidence returning to him.

Her smile never faltering, Aliana gave him the address.

Danno hesitated again. It all seemed like a dream all of a sudden, a wonderful dream that had begun as a nightmare when Danno had learnt about his father's true business. A nightmare that almost got him killed, but one where this beautiful undercover agent was there with him the whole time since he had stepped into the dream.

Aliana nervously bit her lower lip, she was so beautiful when she did that, and Danno's heart fluttered.

'You don't have to be a *perfect* gentleman, you know.'

Danno didn't need telling twice. Placing his hand on her back, Danno pulled Aliana to him for a searing kiss, which she returned just as hungrily. The relief that washed over him was coupled with a desire that blazed within him. Danno inhaled sharply, and exhaled a guttural moan, as his tongue continued to twine with Aliana's.

They pulled away, breathless.

The other agent exaggeratedly minded his own business, but Danno saw him smirking, which made Danno's face feel even hotter.

'I'll see you tonight,' said Danno.

'See you tonight,' Aliana echoed. And in her eyes burned the same desire Danno felt.

Danno slowly backed away, his eyes on Aliana, before turning around, trying to control his impulse to whoop or jump at the thrill of what tonight would offer him. There was a lot to sort out now in his life, and a lot that had gone down badly, but there was a lot of good too. Danno knew he would figure the rest out, with Aliana by his side.

イゴシマ

Igoshima

Katakana is a form of syllabic writing in Japanese.
On the cover of the book is the *Katakana* for
'Igoshima.'

It is written in the *Yokogaki* format –
horizontal, left to right.

The word *igo* means 'surrounding board game.'
The word *shima* means 'island.'

I chose these to create the name for my characters for the symbolism it represents. The island being the legacy, the business, and the mafia. The board game being the playing field – the hotel – where Igoshima Senior and Danno go head to head.

Please enjoy this passage from

Sanguine Sincerity

The first book in an ongoing series of
Supernatural LGBTQ Erotic Romance Thriller
books.

THE EXCERPT IS CLEAN.

Warnings:
Strong language, violence and blood.

<u>Chapter One</u>

Present Day.

The silence was both terrifying and soothing at the same time. Liam closed his eyes and leaned against the brick wall as he stood outside the club. It had been busy, with people dancing, shouting, laughing, all drunkenly. Now, the stillness of the winter night dampened whatever sounds came from the boulevard a few streets down.

This was where he had often stood with Julian after their work shifts, talking, laughing, kissing, and making plans for their future together. But Julian was gone, left before dawn a few nights after they had declared their love for each other, left without a word or explanation. Only a scribble on a sticky note saying, *'I have to leave. I'm sorry.'*

It hurt, it still did, even after all these weeks. Julian had never called or answered Liam's calls or texts after that night; Julian had simply disappeared from Liam's life. Liam didn't understand why – he thought they'd been happy.

He had once relished in the quiet after the bustle of work, now he missed hearing Julian's voice or seeing his smile. His heart broke every day again and again. Yet he continued to stand here in the spot they had made theirs.

Liam couldn't help but wonder if things had moved too fast between them – no, he had declared his love six full months after they'd met and started dating. He was just so confused about it all.

Taking a deep breath, he ensured the club was well locked and began down the dark alley. He didn't want to linger too long. There had been murders in the neighbourhood in recent weeks, all gunshot wounds. The rival gangs were at it again. It hadn't stopped the clubgoers, though. Liam figured it was only a matter of time before both mobs decided they wanted to own the club and took their fight to the neighbouring streets.

Liam heard the screech of tires and shouting not too far. He paused, waiting to make sure it was just some drunk folks, but he tensed when he heard a gunshot pierce the stillness.

Looks like the gang fight's here now, he thought to himself.

He quickened his pace and veered the corner into the next alley and came face to face with the man who had left him.

'Julian!' Liam breathed. He swallowed hard, his heart suddenly drumming in his chest.

'Liam.' Julian hesitated. His blue eyes seemed brighter in the darkness of the night and the light in the alley gave his already pale complexion a blue hue, making his handsome features that much more intense, increasing the yearning and anguish in Liam's heart.

Liam was flooded by a wave of emotions. 'What the hell, Julian?' he shouted, tears stinging his eyes.

Julian winced, chagrined, and Liam saw his eyes sparkle with tears.

'Look,' began Julian, taking a step towards Liam, 'I know I owe you an explanation, I just . . . You need to get out of here. I came to get you to safety.'

Liam took a step back, putting two and two together. 'I know what this is,' he seethed. 'You're with the mafias, aren't you?'

'No, I swear, Liam! I'm not with them,' protested Julian. 'I heard about the Cromwells and Sharpes taking their fight here and I came to warn you. Liam, please.' Julian reached for Liam's hand.

Liam pulled away out of reach. 'A little convenient, isn't it?'

Julian grimaced. 'Liam, I promise you—'

'Promise me? I told you I loved you and then you ran!' shouted Liam, his voice hoarse with heartache. His heart felt tight, and it hurt all over again.

Julian merely gaped at him.

'I thought you loved me too,' Liam wept.

'I do. I do *still* love you,' insisted Julian.

'Then why did you leave?' demanded Liam.

'I had . . . priorities.' He caught himself. 'Sorry, that sounds . . . I had . . . a mission.'

'A mission?' Liam repeated, incredulous. 'Crime mission? Or are you with the cops?'

'None of those,' admitted Julian. 'Look, I promise I'll explain everything. Let's just get out of here, go somewhere safe, and I'll explain everything.' He paused and a tear trickled down his cheek – he wiped it away with the back of his thumb. 'I just ask that you trust me.'

'You left, Julian.' The tightness in Liam's chest squeezed harder. 'You claim you love me but you left – why come back now?'

Julian stared at Liam, eyes pleading. 'I had no choice, something . . . took me away for a while, and I realise I should have told you then what it was and why that was, because—'

Gunshot thundering too close for comfort interrupted their tearful exchange.

Julian grabbed Liam's hand and began to run, pulling Liam along with him. 'We have to get out of here. I'm not going to let any harm come to you.'

'Oh, how noble!' spat Liam.

Julian spun on Liam, glaring at him. 'I came back as soon as my mission was complete. I always intended to. I just couldn't tell you then and it's . . . difficult to explain, it would be difficult for you to belie—'

With surprising speed, Julian placed his hand in front of Liam and pushed him against the wall, backing up as a bullet whizzed past them.

Liam stared at Julian, mouth agape. 'Thanks.'

Julian took a beat, looking alarmed, before grabbing hold of Liam's hand again and guiding him out of the alley and bolting onto the street. Shouts coming from nearby told them which way *not* to run as they turned onto the next street over, darting as fast as they could.

Some of the mobsters ran onto the street where they were. Julian skidded to a stop, his eyes darting this way and that, looking hypervigilant. He grabbed Liam's arm and pulled him close, turning around as one of the gang members took aim at them. They ducked behind a parked car.

'We're not with the Sharpes!' Julian shouted. Liam noted how Julian had easily recognised that the ones shooting at them were the Cromwells.

In response, the shooter reloaded his gun.

'Shit!' Julian cursed. He looked towards another parked car. 'If we can get ourselves out of this area,' he told Liam, 'then we—'

The window of the car behind which they hid shattered as another shot resounded behind them.

They ran towards the next car, and then towards another building. Another thunderous roar broke the air as more gang members began shooting at each other. Liam and Julian's assailant continued after them and just as they came up to hide in an alcove, a bullet hit Julian with a thud.

He cried out in pain, bringing his hand to his arm.

'Julian!' Liam cried.

Julian closed his eyes, wincing. 'I'll be fine,' he gritted. He looked over at Liam as they leaned against the wall. 'I'm sorry I never told you the truth. I'm sorry

I left – I'm sorry I hurt you. But I swear I love you and I will tell you *everything*. We just need to get to safety.'

Liam nodded. 'You knew they were coming here. I just can't wrap my head around—'

'I found out just hours ago.' Julian looked at his wound, breathing deeply but looking like the pain wasn't as intense now as it was before. 'I got myself here as quickly as I could.'

'You came to . . . warn me . . .' Liam was just so confused. 'Please, tell me if you're part of a gang of some sort.'

'Of some sort,' Julian repeated pensively. 'Not a mafia, no. Not a . . . It's complicated.' Julian pinched his fingers and reached into his wound and pulled out the bullet with nothing more than a small groan. 'I'm good.'

Suddenly, the barrel of a handgun emerged from the corner – the shooter was pointing it straight at Julian's head, his grip on the handgun firm and steady.

Liam froze.

Julian stared the other man in the eyes. 'Big mistake,' he sneered.

With exceptional speed, he grabbed the assailant's arm, pulling and twisting. The Cromwell crony cried out, dropping the gun, and Julian grabbed his neck and twisted hard. The man fell dead on the ground before him.

Liam stared at Julian. 'And you say you're not a cop or with a mob,' he said, unconvinced. He pointed at the dead shooter, his eyes never leaving Julian's. 'Explain that!'

'Not here.'

Julian picked up the dead man's gun and began to run; Liam followed close behind. A car turned onto the street and mobsters began to shoot at anyone who was nearby.

'Fuck!' Julian shouted. Shielding Liam as they continued to run, Julian took aim and began shooting at the mobsters within the vehicle, hitting his mark every time.

'Now I know there's definitely something you're not telling me,' Liam muttered as they ran.

'There is, and I promise I'll tell you,' replied Julian. He secured the clip and aimed afresh, again not missing his target.

Liam's throat and lungs were burning but he pushed forward. They turned another corner as the car behind them crashed into a fence.

Liam stopped before Julian, facing him. 'The truth now, Julian!'

Panting, Julian stared at Liam. 'We need to get away from here,' he insisted.

'I'm not moving until you tell me what's going on.'

Fear flashed in Julian's eyes. 'You're not going to believe me without the full explanation.'

'Then quit stalling and explain already!' demanded Liam.

Julian worked his jaw. 'I'm—'

A deafening gunshot exploded – Liam felt a sharp, burning sensation in his gut, and his knees buckled beneath him as he struggled to stay upright.

'No!' screamed Julian.

He caught Liam before he could hit the ground, gently setting him down. Liam's breath came out syncopated as he realised what had just happened. He screamed in pain – a loud guttural scream – then winced, clenching his jaw.

'No, no, this is what I was trying to prevent,' Julian quavered, opening up Liam's jacket and staring at the wound. 'I can't lose you.'

'Lose me? You left me.'

Julian let out a tearful breath. 'I left on a mission I couldn't tell you about. I'm so sorry, Liam.'

Liam glanced down at his stomach as his blood rapidly drenched his clothes. Seeing it only made his heart pump harder and the blood gush faster, and Liam's breath came out shakily.

Julian pulled Liam close to his chest, picking him up off the ground, and began to run. Liam didn't know if it was the dizziness of blood loss that altered his perceptions but he felt like they were moving a lot faster than was normal. He saw houses whizz by his vision and then trees as they entered the forest. The sounds of guns and shouting mobsters grew distant until, finally, the quiet of the night was all that remained.

Julian placed Liam down on the snow, which quickly turned red from his blood. Julian's jaw was clenched.

The pain Liam felt was immeasurable, yet somehow he couldn't bring himself to scream again, and he was so sweat-soaked from fear, he barely noticed the cold.

'I should never have waited this long to tell you the truth, Liam.' Julian looked down at Liam's wound, his tears dripping onto it.

Liam tried to speak but a mere whimper escaped him as tears stung his eyes.

Julian's voice came out determined yet half-whispered. 'I'm not going to let you die.'

'I think,' Liam winced, his voice laboured, 'it's too late for that.'

'No!' Something flashed in Julian's eyes. Liam lifted a bloodied hand to Julian's face; Julian placed his hand on his. 'I came back because I love you . . . because I owe you the truth. So here is the truth.'

His eyes flashed again and paled, brightening, his pupils becoming as blue as his irises and nearly as pale. He let his mouth hang open, and smoothly his top canines extended. Liam's eyes widened and he gaped at Julian.

'You're a—' he gasped.

'Yes. I can save your life, but tell me no and I won't, as much as that grieves me. I won't force this life on you.'

Liam gritted his teeth as a wave of pain threatened to pull him into unconsciousness. 'Do it!'

Julian leaned down towards him and gently placed his teeth on his skin. He paused. Liam felt Julian's breath on his neck before an intense sting.

He winced, grabbing Julian's arm tightly. He felt Julian's lips wrap around the punctures and the pain eased. As Julian sucked his blood, Liam relaxed in his caress.

Julian kissed Liam's neck tenderly before pulling away. 'It's done,' he said softly.

Liam waited, his body trembling lightly. Then he began to shake, but not from pain, from some sort of power that coursed through his veins. It was a vibration that came from inside of him that he felt gushing through all his veins. In his mouth, Liam felt his eyeteeth extend, and there was a mild prickle in his eyes that he just knew was the same kind of flare he'd seen in Julian's eyes.

Liam looked down at his wound, feeling an uncomfortable sensation. The bullet appeared at the opening of the hole in his stomach and fell out. Then the wound closed and Liam felt himself heal inside his body. It wasn't pleasant but the discomfort quickly passed.

Liam swallowed hard, breathing in deeply. He stared at Julian.

He wasn't sure which of them sprung towards the other first but their lips met and their mouths opened to let the other in, and they kissed fervently. The familiar tingling in Liam's stomach told him how much he loved and wanted Julian.

He pulled away. Julian leaned his forehead on his.

'I am so sorry, Liam, that I never told you the truth.'

'You should have trusted that I'd believe you,' Liam placed his hand on Julian's face, 'that I'd still love you despite who or what you are.' Liam grimaced at the blood he'd smeared on Julian who didn't seem to mind.

Julian kissed Liam again. 'I love you, Liam. I promise I'll never leave your side again.'

Liam let that sink in, realising the implications of this new situation. 'I guess that means we're geared to spend eternity together.'

Julian's lips quirked into a side grin. 'Is that a proposal?'

Liam chuckled, feeling flutters all over his body. 'It is if you want it to be.'

Julian beamed at him, and with his heightened senses Liam could feel the truth and their love reverberate and pulse between them.

Liam pressed a long and ardent kiss to Julian's lips, wrapping his arms around him, deepening the kiss with each passing moment, and his tongue traced his lover's vampiric canines as they hungrily devoured each other's mouths.

Liam drew back and met Julian's gaze. 'You owe me one hell of an explanation.'

Julian let out a small laugh. 'That, I do.'

Julian helped Liam to his feet and he beckoned him to follow. He held out his hand and Liam took it, interlacing their fingers. They walked through the snow in the forest, the silence of the night no longer terrifying Liam, and Julian's voice soothingly cut through the stillness as he began his story.

Also By

Also Written by Eidahs

Sanguine Sincerity
(https://binkyproductions.com/supernaturalromance)

Like Father, Not Like Sons
(www.binkyproductions.com/shortstories)

Also Published by Binky Ink

Stardust Destinies I: Variate Facing
Stardust Destinies II: The Drought
(https://binkyproductions.com/stardustdestinies)

Multiple Short Stories on Medium
Soon To Be Published in Book Format
(https://medium.com/@BinkyInkWriting)

Eidahs is a pseudonym for all mature written works, from thrillers to erotic romance. Eidahs in pronunciation sounds elven in nature, which is why she chose it, to tap into her love of fantasy, a genre that couples well with supernatural and preternatural, dark fantasy, and romance.

Eidahs is also the nickname 'Shadie' backwards, representing the shadow self, innermost desires, and a spectrum of emotions, most notably, passion, sorrow, rage, and delight, which Eidahs loves to incorporate in her writing. Enticing readers and evoking the characters' emotions when she writes has guided her inspiration to spell many short stories on Medium and a series of books under this pen name.

Connect with Binky Ink:

WordPress Website & Blog
    https://binkyproductions.com/binkyinkwriting
Medium – Main Profile
    https://medium.com/@BinkyInkWriting
X (Twitter) https://twitter.com/binkyinkwriting

* 9 7 8 1 7 3 8 2 8 2 9 2 0 *